W9-BRJ-931

WILLIE
JEROME

WILLIE JEROME

BY ALICE FAYE DUNCAN

ILLUSTRATED BY
TYRONE GETER

Macmillan Books for Young Readers • New York

Macmillan Books for Young Readers
An imprint of Simon & Schuster Children's Publishing Division

Simon & Schuster Macmillan
1230 Avenue of the Americas
New York, New York 10020

The text of this book is set in Garamond Book.
The illustrations were done in oil paints.
Printed and bound in Hong Kong on recycled paper.

First edition
10 9 8 7 6 5 4 3 2 1

LIBRARY OF CONGRESS CATALOGING-IN-PUBLICATION DATA
Duncan, Alice Faye.
Willie Jerome / Alice Faye Duncan ; illustrated by Tyrone Geter.
— 1st ed.
p. cm.
Summary: Nobody appreciates Willie Jerome's jazz trumpet playing
except his sister, who finally makes Mama listen to the music speak.
ISBN 0-02-733208-X
[1. Jazz—Fiction. 2. Brothers and sisters—Fiction. 3. Afro-
Americans—Fiction.] I. Geter, Tyrone, ill. II. Title.
PZ7.D8947Wi 1995
[E]—dc20 94-10444

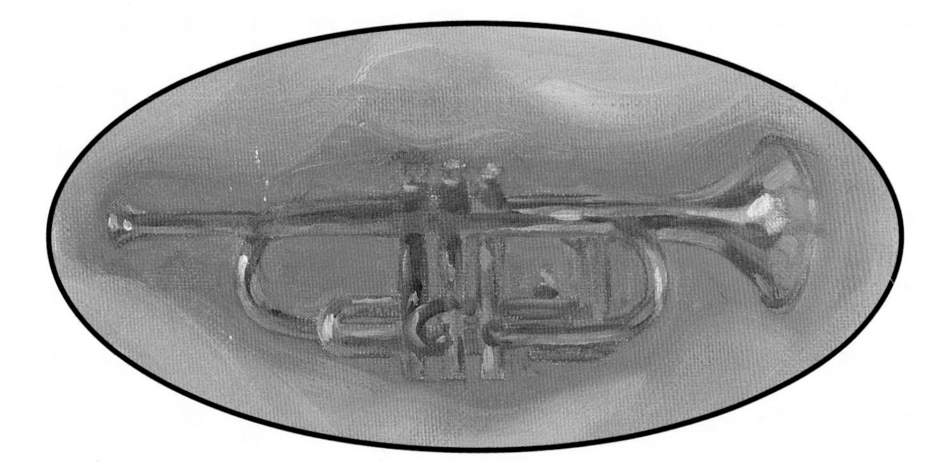

For Joia Maria Brown
and
Kenneth Duncan Jr.
—A. F. D.

To the talented children of the world.
Let them always have the opportunity to grow, develop,
and above all, create.
—T. G.

TOYS

When summer comes,
Willie Jerome plays jazz
on the rooftop
all day long.

Mama say he be up there making noise.
I say he be up there making music.
Mama say, “Willie Jerome better be off that roof
when I come home this evening.”

My big brother, Earl,
who talk all bad and mean,
say that Willie Jerome
ain't got no talent.
He say, "He need to
put that trumpet down."

I get Earl told.
I get Earl told, quick.
I say, "Willie Jerome
on the rooftop
playing sizzlin'
red hot bebop,
and I like it.
I like it a lot."

"Sizzlin' red hot bebop?" ask Earl.
"Crazy girl, you can't hear.
Willie Jerome up there making noise,
while you walking 'round calling it music."

FIRE

I dismiss Earl
and trot on across
to the corner store.
Mr. Jackson peeps
the groove in my stride.
He wanna know why
I'm smiling so.

"Willie Jerome
on the rooftop," I say.
"I been groovin' to
his noonday songs.
That's why I got this
smile on my face.
That's why I got this
bop in my stride."

Mr. Jackson hands me some candy
in exchange for my shiny quarter.
Then he looks out at Willie Jerome
on the rooftop. He shakes his head
like it's a crying shame.
"Little Miss Judy," he say to me.
"I hate to tell ya the bad news.
But Willie Jerome can't play no trumpet.
That boy up there just making noise."

I walk out the store and head for home.
I bop on back to my front stoop.
That's when I see Miss Alversa Lee,
watering the green plants in her window.

"Hey-hey there, Miss Alversa Lee.
You liking Willie Jerome's jazz music?"

"Honey, naw!" she yells down.
"I'm not liking it one bit.
So do Miss Alversa Lee a favor,
go tell Willie Jerome
to hush wit' all that racket."

I start to feel sorta blue
'cause don't nobody seem to care
for Willie Jerome's rooftop music
except me, myself, and him.

"Willie Jerome!" I shout.
"Willie Jerome, I just wish I knew
another somebody who loves and understands
your sizzlin' hot jazz the way I do."

Willie Jerome is a boy of very few words.
So he don't answer back or nothing.
Instead, he just keeps digging on his horn
and moving back and forth with the music.

Around six o’clock,
Mama get home from work,
and she frown this ugly frown
’cause Willie Jerome
still on the rooftop
playing that bebop,
and Mama tired.
She don’t wanna
hear his noise.

“I’m going up to the rooftop,” say Mama.
“I’m gonna put an end to this.”
But I quickly catch her hand
and ask her to wait a minute.

“Don’t bother Willie Jerome,” I plead.
“Just close your eyes. Rest your mind, and
let the music speak to your spirit.”

So Mama loosens up her frown
and takes a seat by me on the stoop.
We close our eyes.
We rest our minds and
let the music speak.

As the evening sun begins to set,
Willie plays his last sweet melody.